The Gold in the Grave

in the Grave

Terry Deary

Illustrated by Helen Flook

A&C Black • London

First published 2004 by
A & C Black Publishers Ltd
37 Soho Square, London W1D 3QZ
www.acblack.com

Text copyright © 2004 Terry Deary
Illustrations copyright © 2004 Helen Flook

The rights of Terry Deary and Helen Flook to be identified
as the author and illustrator of this work respectively have been
asserted by them in accordance with the Copyrights, Designs
and Patents Act 1988.

ISBN 0-7136-7001-0

A CIP catalogue for this book is available from the
British Library.

A & C Black uses paper produced with elemental
chlorine-free pulp, harvested from managed sustainable forests.

Printed and bound in Spain by G. Z. Printek, Bilbao.

Chapter 1

The Perfect Plot

The eve of the robbery…

The water clock dripped. It was the second hour of the afternoon and time to go. Time to carry out the greatest robbery in the history of the world.

There were four of us in the room. Four grave robbers. And we had the perfect plot.

They had been burying kings in Egypt for thousands of years. Burying them with gold and jewels to spend in the Afterlife.

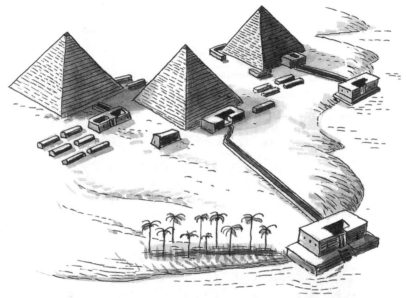

And people had been robbing those kings for thousands of years, to spend the fortunes in *this* life. Kings were buried in pyramids to guard their gold.

It didn't work.

No one used pyramids any more. They were too easy to rob. Now the kings were buried in tombs. Deep in the rocky cliffs near Thebes. There was only one way in – and that was guarded.

Dalifa was the temple jeweller who made ornaments for King Tutankhamen's tomb.

Antef was the master thief, the greatest tomb robber in the world.

"I have saved a lot of money," he said.
"Now I am going to risk it all to win the
biggest prize of all. And you are going to
help me." He chuckled and showed his
black and yellow stumps of teeth.

At least that was the idea. If we could
rob the tomb of King Tutankhamen then
we would be rich as kings. If we failed
then our punishment would be horrible –
so horrible it gave me nightmares.

Big Kerpes
would be one
of the coffin
carriers at the
sunset funeral of
Tutankhamen.

Tutankhamen had been dead for seventy days. Days spent in turning his holy body into a mummy. From the first day of the King's death, Antef had been plotting the perfect plot.

Kerpes told me, "If they catch you they'll cut off your nose." He rubbed his own flat broken, nose. "If you are lucky."

"And if I am unlucky?" I asked.

"Then the new King Ay will have you crucified – nailed to the walls of Thebes city. He will show the world what happens to grave robbers."

"I don't want to be nailed to the wall, Kerpes," I whispered.

"Then don't get caught," he grunted.

Me? I am Paneb. In those days I was the poor son of a tavern owner. I wasn't very clever and I wasn't very brave. But I was very, very skinny. And that's why they wanted me.

Antef had come to me in my father's tavern where I was gathering pots. He knew I was a thief. I would steal anything – from washing on the riverbank where it was stretched out to dry, to food in the temple laid out for the gods.

"The plan is simple but brilliant," he told me. "The King's tomb is waiting for him in an underground cave across the river. He will be buried there with his fortune in seventy days time."

"And guarded," I said. "We can't get in."

He gave his gap-toothed grin again. "We don't have to. We just have to get *out*!"

"Uh?"

"The King will be placed in the tomb then the door will be sealed. But *you* will already be in there. On the inside. Hiding," he said. "We'll slip you in before the funeral."

I shuddered. "I'll be trapped in the tomb – in the dark – with the dead King and all the spirits? The door is a huge slab of stone. I won't be able to break out. I'll die."

He shook his head. "I have friends in the stone quarry. They have made the door. One corner has been cracked and put back with weak mortar. You can't see the fault unless you know it is there. You smash open the corner and pass out the King's fortune."

It was a clever plan. "How do I get in?"

"You go to the scribe school by the temple. The scribe master is a friend of mine. He will train you as a scribe, and you will be sent into the tomb to paint the prayers on the walls. The guards will get used to seeing you," he promised.

"So, after the funeral, I have to pass the treasure out through the corner of the door. You'll be waiting in the passage?" I asked.

"Yes."

"But the passage will be guarded," I argued. "If you can't get down to the door I'll be trapped alone."

"I have used most of my money to pay the guards," he said. "They will look the other way. And you will not be alone. Dalifa will be with you."

I looked at the girl who sat quietly chewing a date. She was dressed as a priestess.

My partner in crime.

Chapter 2

The Temple Trick

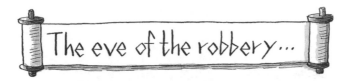

The eve of the robbery...

Antef smiled across at Dalifa and asked her, "How did you get on in the temple?"

Dalifa looked sour. "I had to wear a lot of uncomfortable clothes and do some disgusting things," she said. "I mean to say, I get my meat from a butcher in the market … when I can afford it."

We nodded. I usually ate bread and onions but I had tasted meat. When I was rich – after the robbery – I would eat meat every day.

"But I've never had to kill my own meat!" Dalifa said.

"The priests made you kill something before you could eat it?" I asked.

She turned her narrow eyes on me with scorn. "You are as stupid as Kerpes," she snarled. "Every day they sacrifice a kid goat to the god Osiris. They gave me a live goat and told me to cut its throat, collect the blood in a bowl and cook the rest."

"Did you do it?" I asked.

"I did not," she said. "I took the goat to the butcher and swapped it for a bowl of blood and some cooked goat meat. The priests never knew."

"Did Osiris drink the blood?" I wanted to know.

Dalifa clenched her hands. "Osiris ... is ... a ... stone ... statue, Paneb. They make sacrifices to him and the peasants think Osiris drinks the blood, but he doesn't."

"So, who eats the cooked meat?" I asked.

Dalifa spread her hands. "The priests, of course! They have it for their evening meal."

"Poor Osiris must get hungry," I said.

"He ... is ... a ... stone ... oh, never mind!" Dalifa snapped.

Then she realised I was teasing and gave me a look as bitter as cobra venom.

"But the plot," Antef reminded her. "Did you get a job in the funeral of King Tutankhamen?"

Dalifa nodded once. "I travel with the funeral all the way. From the temple, over the river and all the way to the tomb."

"Ahh!" Antef breathed. "That is another piece of the plot in place."

"Then I hope I never have to go back to that blood-soaked temple again," Dalifa said. "The chief priest of Osiris is a terrifying man – and this morning he reminded us all of the hideous punishments we would suffer if there is a theft at the funeral."

Even Antef looked worried. But not as worried as when a shadow blocked the light from the doorway and a soldier stood there.

Chapter 3

The Grim Guard

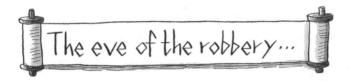

The eve of the robbery...

The soldier was even larger than Kerpes. His face was scarred from battle blows and his voice was harsh as a vulture's cry.

"Antef – grave robber. I want a word with you and your friends."

"We've done nothing!" Antef said quickly.

"Tutankhamen's widow has sent me to check on all the grave robbers of Thebes. So what are you plotting?" the soldier asked.

Antef shrugged. "The boy was just showing us how the walls of the tomb are painted," he said.

"So show me," the soldier said and he knelt beside me.

The soldier picked up my sketch. I hadn't had time to hide it. "This looks like a plan of the King's tomb, Antef," he said.

"Really!" The old man gasped. "You surprise me, soldier."

The man clutched at his knife and straightened. "I am Khammale and I am not a simple soldier. I am captain of the palace guard."

"Sorry, officer," Antef smiled.

"I saw that idle Kerpes leave here a few moments ago. What part is he in the plot?" Khammale asked. "Coffin carrier?"

Antef tried to answer but, if he was like me, his mouth was too dry to speak. Dry with fear because Captain Khammale had already guessed that part of our plot.

He went on, "And I suppose the boy is a scribe who went in to the tomb to spy out the plan? The girl here will be a priestess, I expect."

"No!" Dalifa said. "I made some of the ornaments that will be going in the tomb."

"Shut up, Dalifa!" Antef said savagely. "The good officer doesn't want to know about that!"

"Oh, but I do," Captain Khammale said.

Dalifa smiled and said, "I've always made ornaments and little statues. So, of course, I was happy to offer my skills to the priests to make ornaments for Tutankhamen's tomb."

Captain Khammale nodded. "Now you will help Antef to take them out again. Melt the gold and silver down and make new ones to sell and make your fortune!"

"No!" Antef said. "We would never rob the grave of our dear, dead King. Never!"

"Good," Captain Khammale grinned. "Because if you try it, and if I catch you, I will tie you to a tree, then I will cut off your ears and then your nose. Then I will cut off little strips of skin one at a time and pour salt water into the cuts. Then I will let the ants and the jackals finish you off."

"Would you like that, Antef?"

The old man shook his head. My own mouth felt as dry as dust at the horror of the thought. The Captain rose and left.

"We can't go ahead now," I said.

Antef looked at the empty doorway. "Oh, yes we can, Paneb. I have spent all my money on this plot. There is no turning back now."

In the warm room I shivered.

Chapter 4

The Terrible Trap

"Antef," I snivelled, "I don't want to have my ears cut off! I'd scream!"

Dalifa threw her head back and laughed. "If your ears were cut off you wouldn't hear yourself!"

"It's not funny," I shouted.

The old man reached across, grabbed my tunic and hissed, "Captain Khammale was just guessing. He knows nothing. Anyway, he is just one man. He can't stop us."

Dalifa scoffed, "Paneb's frightened."

"You will have Dalifa with you. Think of the riches waiting for you," Antef breathed.

Dalifa smiled at me and said, "I have seen those riches, Paneb," she said proudly. "One golden servant for each day of the year and enough jewellery to break a camel's back," she went on.

"Kerpes and I will be waiting at the end of the tunnel with some strong men to carry it all to the boat." Antef added.

I blinked. "Tunnel? What tunnel? It's just a door into a passage. I pass the goods through a door."

"The King will be placed in his coffins – he has three of them," Antef explained. "Then the priests will sweep the floor and leave. They will close the door to the tomb and seal it. The King's workers will fill in the passage with stones to block it off."

"I'll be sealed behind a stone door and a passage full of stones? I can't dig my way out!" I argued.

"We will dig our way in," Antef said. That is why we have the stupid, but strong, Kerpes."

"I don't want to be shut in a tomb!" I wailed.

"It will only be for the night," Antef said. "We'll start digging a tunnel as soon as the workmen leave. We will pay the guards to look the other way. You'll be out as the sun rises."

"We'll take the treasures in a boat down the river. There are traders there waiting to buy them from us," Dalifa said.

"Just one day from now you will have more riches than you could earn in your lifetime as a peasant farmer."

"It's not the day I'm worried about. It's the night," I told them.

Antef laughed. He gripped my arm in his claw hand. "Time to take the boat," he said.

We stepped into the quiet streets.

"Everyone has gone to see the procession," Dalifa said, nodding towards the temple. "Time for me to join it." Dalifa waved goodbye.

Antef and I hurried down to the riverside where the huge barges were waiting to take Tutankhamen on his last voyage.

I just hoped it wouldn't be my last voyage too.

Chapter 5

To the Tomb

The eve of the robbery...

We slid over the water faster than a fish and landed on the western shore. The west where the sun set and where Tutankhamen's spirit would soon be travelling ... without his treasure.

The evening sun was cool as we crossed the desert. This was the road I'd taken every day for seventy days to Tutankhamen's tomb. I knew the way. But usually I walked with the other young scribes and our masters and a few of the royal archers.

Desert lions and jackals never troubled us and the archers would drive them off if they did.

But this evening Antef and I were alone and the cries of the creatures made our feet shuffle along the road as fast as our racing heartbeats.

Great piles of gravel stood by the entrance to the tomb. "That is ready to shovel in once the King is inside," Antef said.

"And me – they'll block me in too."

"Not for long," Antef said with a wink. "These stone workers are friends of mine. They will not fill it to the roof. We'll have you out in a couple of hours." He waved to one of the labourers who leaned on his shovel.

A guard blocked the door. He was there every day and he knew my face. That's what Antef had been hoping for. "The boy has come to finish the painting," the old man explained.

"A bit late," the guard grumbled. He looked across the desert to a cloud of dust that was rolling in from the river. The funeral parade. "They're almost here."

Antef turned on me and acted angry. "See, stupid boy? I told you this should have been finished yesterday." He slapped me with a horny hand and drove me into the corridor. "These boys are a waste of time!" he called as he passed the guard.

Servants and priests and craftsmen and scribes were in the tomb putting everything in its place, ready to receive the King.

I knew the room where Antef wanted me to hide. We passed through the entrance chamber where a golden chariot was lying in pieces on the floor. The King's servants would have to put it together to drive him into the Afterlife.

The light from the oil lamps glittered on all that gold. Gold everywhere, above my head and beneath my feet. I was dazzled by gold and my greed made me almost faint.

I slipped through the door into the back chamber that was packed with treasure and Antef began to close it behind me. "When the funeral arrives stay silent," he warned.

The door closed with a thud that sounded as hollow as my lonely heart felt.

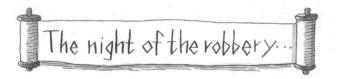
It was cool in the chamber, not cold. But I shivered. Gods and ghosts were haunting me. I swear they were there in the shadows.

I heard the workmen finish in the vault outside. Then a lot of noise as the funeral procession arrived and the priests placed the King in his coffins.

Then I heard a softer sound nearby as the door to my hiding place slid open. I crouched behind a large model boat. And waited for the thrust of a guard's sword. Instead I heard the hiss, "Paneb? Are you there?"

It was Dalifa. She closed the door quickly and gave me her sharp-eyed look. She whispered. "The funeral is over. They'll be sealing the tomb ... listen!"

I strained my ears. Suddenly the door swung open and lamplight spilled in. A guard stuck his head around the door and looked at us. I groaned. Nailed to the walls of Thebes, I knew it. I knew it would all go wrong.

The guard raised his lamp and grinned. "Are you all right, kids?" he asked.

"Kerpes?"

Dalifa hissed. "Go away baboon-brain."

The big man frowned. "Sorry. Just thought I'd see if you were comfortable."

"We'll all be comfortable nailed to the walls of Thebes," she spat. "Get out!"

"See you in the morning," the flat-nosed man said and closed the door. His footsteps clumped away.

After a while it was silent – silent as a grave! Dalifa gave a sharp nod. "Right, we are shut in. Start opening boxes and filling these pouches."

She lit an oil lamp and handed me some linen bags and began to fill them with golden arm bands and statues, jewels and rings.

I scrabbled in the wooden cases and came up with more. We moved out into the entry chamber and then into the burial room itself. Soon we had twenty bags filled with treasures.

Dalifa turned to the door and began to scrape at a crack in the top corner with her dagger. The corner broke off as Antef meant it to and there was just enough room for someone small like me or Dalifa to crawl through. But the far side was already blocked with small stones and they fell in on our heads.

"What if Antef doesn't come back for us?" I asked.

Dalifa pointed at the treasure. "For this Antef will chew his way through the stone. Be patient!"

And so we waited through the long night. Slowly I slipped into sleep. I awoke when stones fell through the broken corner of the door and Antef's face stared through.

"Time to go!" he said.

Chapter 6

The Face of Death

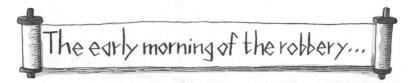

The early morning of the robbery...

I passed one of the bags to Antef and then helped Dalifa up to the opening. I crawled after her, clutching a bag full of rings. I stuffed it into my belt so I could use my hands to pull myself along.

Sharp stones scraped at my knees and elbows and the dust choked my throat and stung my eyes.

At last I felt the cool morning air on my face and blinked into the sunlight. Big Kerpes stood there, filthy from the digging but looking pleased. Antef was staring into his treasure bag, eyes alight with the morning sun.

Dalifa stretched out a hand for my treasure. I put my hand to my belt. The bag of rings had gone. It had fallen from my belt as I'd crawled along. We needed to make a few journeys. I'd find it later, I thought.

Then I looked up to the bank over the top of the entrance passage. A woman stood there. She wore a plain white gown and a rich wig. Her sweet perfume drifted down to me. She was the most beautiful thing I'd ever seen in my young life.

My mouth fell open. The others saw me staring and turned to look. Antef gave a soft moan.

There was a rattle of stones as a man in heavy sandals appeared behind the lady. He said, "Don't you peasants kneel when you come before your Queen Ankhesenamen?"

It was Captain Khammale of the palace guard. We fell to our knees in front of Tutankhamen's widow.

"I will have sharp wooden stakes put up by the river," the captain said to the Queen. "I will have the thieves dropped on to the stakes to show all of Thebes what happens to grave robbers." His eyes were bright with the thought of our deaths.

The queen spoke quietly. "No, Khammale. No more deaths. My husband died for the treasures of Egypt. These poor people need not die."

The joy slipped from the face of Captain Khammale. "They must be punished, your Highness."

The sad-faced queen spread her hands. "They hoped to steal a life of laziness," she sighed. "So punish them with a life of work. Set them to work in the fields. I will take the girl to be a handmaiden in my palace."

Dalifa smirked. It was more a reward than a punishment.

"She will scrub and sew until her fingers bleed," Ankhesenamen promised.

Dalifa's smirk slid from her face.

The Captain shook his head. "As you wish, your Highness."

He drew his sword and held it at Antef's throat. "To the river you filthy little thief." He looked at me. "And you too, boy."

He pointed at big Kerpes. "And as for you, you can start filling in that tunnel."

The day after the robbery...

At noon the next day the sun was high and even the crocodiles were too hot to move from the river. But we were working on the shadufs and the fields, pulling at weeds until our backs were breaking and sweat flowed like the Nile.

Just one day before, I had been dreaming of a life of ease and more riches than I could ever spend. One dreadful day later and I had only a nightmare of work and poverty.

The guards let us stop to drink a little weak beer and chew on an onion each. "We were wrong to try and rob the dead, Antef," I moaned as I sank to the ground beside him.

He looked at me quickly. "No. We were not wrong. The only thing we did wrong was getting caught. There was nothing *wrong* with trying to make ourselves rich."

I looked across the fields to the royal palace. "Even the Queen didn't look happy with all her riches," I said.

Antef snorted. "No. They say the new king is Ay, Tutankhamen's uncle. To make the throne his own he will marry little widow-Queen Ankhesenamen."

"He's an old man," I said. "Poor lady."

Antef looked up and slapped my aching shoulders with his horny hand. "He is old! Hah! There's a thought, Paneb!"

"So?"

"So ... he will die soon. And when he does, they will bury him with all his wealth. And next time we'll be more careful. We'll make sure we aren't caught!"

A guard cracked a whip and ordered us back to the baked fields.

"Next time?"

Antef grinned his broken-toothed grin. "Next time," he chuckled. "Next time."

Afterword

By 1900 all the kings' tombs of ancient Egypt had been robbed. Some had been robbed soon after the king was buried, some were robbed in modern times.

Then, in 1922, the archaeologist Howard Carter came across a forgotten tomb – the tomb of a young king called Tutankhamen. It was full of the dead King's treasure. But there was a mystery. A tunnel had been dug from the door of the tomb to the outside. In the tunnel was a bag of rings. Someone had broken in to the tomb soon after the king was buried over 3,200 years before.

They must have been caught because the tunnel was filled in and the treasures saved.

How did the robbery and the arrest happen? We'll never know. *The Gold in the Grave* is a guess. But it *could* have happened that way.

Most ancient Egyptian graves were robbed by the people who built them or people who paid the guards to let them in. The robbers worked in gangs and had ways of selling their treasure quickly.

The other mystery is how young Tutankhamen died. Modern x-rays of his mummy show he seems to have had a bang on the head. Did he fall? Or was he murdered?

Egyptian Tales